nickelodeon

SPONGEBOB SQUAREPANTS

SPONGE SAVES THE DAY!

SIMON SPOTLIGHT/NICKELODEON

New York   London   Toronto   Sydney   New Delhi

Stephen Hillenburg

Based on the TV series *SpongeBob SquarePants*™ created by Stephen Hillenburg as seen on Nickelodeon™

SIMON SPOTLIGHT/NICKELODEON

An imprint of Simon & Schuster Children's Publishing Division

1230 Avenue of the Americas, New York, New York 10020

SpongeBob to the Rescue! © 2010 Viacom International Inc.

The Great Patty Caper © 2010 Viacom International Inc.

Legends of Bikini Bottom © 2011 Viacom International Inc.

SIMON SPOTLIGHT and colophon are registered trademarks of Simon & Schuster, Inc.

For information about special discounts for bulk purchases, please contact Simon & Schuster Special Sales at 1-866-506-1949 or business@simonandschuster.com.

Manufactured in the United States of America 0612 LAK

ISBN 978-1-4424-6642-5

These titles were previously published individually by Simon Spotlight.

by Alison Inches
illustrated by Gibbs Rainock

On the way home from work SpongeBob spied something by the side of the road. "Wow, an old propeller!" he exclaimed. "This will make a *great* lawn ornament! Hmm, I never realized how much neat stuff people leave lying around."

So SpongeBob picked up the propeller and headed home.

The next day SpongeBob brought home an old tire, a forgotten laundry basket, and a worn-out boot. Patrick and Gary stared at the pile of junk.

"This must be my lucky week!" SpongeBob told them. "I can turn this old tire into a swing and this laundry basket into a playpen for Gary."

"Meow," said Gary.

"Sorry, Gary," said SpongeBob. "Not a playpen—I meant luxury snail house."

"But, SpongeBob, it's just a bunch of junk!" Patrick exclaimed.

"Patrick, my friend," said SpongeBob, "you may see junk, but I see possibilities. Haven't you heard the old saying, 'One man's junk is another man's treasure'?"

"Ooh, is it a pirate treasure?" Patrick asked with newfound excitement.

Everywhere SpongeBob went he kept an eye out for junk. He checked the gutters. He looked in the storm drains. He combed the beach at Goo Lagoon. SpongeBob found everything from empty soda cans to plastic milk jugs.

"Hello there, ginormous clam!" said SpongeBob as he walked past. "Are you going to eat that bottle cap in your shell?"

The giant clam shook his head no, and SpongeBob plucked the cap out of his shell.

Then SpongeBob passed a dolphin tangled in an old fishing net.

"Hey, friend!" called SpongeBob. "May I have that net when you're done playing with it?"

The dolphin struggled this way and that as he tried to free himself.

"I'll take that as a yes!" said SpongeBob, and he untangled the dolphin.

"Thanks, pal," said the dolphin as he swam away.

"No, no! Thank *you!*" said SpongeBob. "This fishing net will make a perfect hammock for my backyard!"

Over the next week SpongeBob's junk collection grew and grew.

"Gee, Gary," said SpongeBob. "I better organize this stuff until I can make good use of it all. It's beginning to take over the house."

SpongeBob bought several bins, labeled them, and placed them outside his house.

"Junk, sweet junk!" sang SpongeBob as he organized. "The possibilities are endless. Junk can become art, or a place to sit, or a pretty decoration. . . ."

"Or a total EYESORE!" yelled Squidward, who had stopped to have a look.

"It's not an eyesore, it's my treasure!" SpongeBob replied. "Someday this junk will be worth something!"

"Worth something!" exclaimed Squidward, laughing. "Hmm, let me see. A pile of junk plus a pile of junk equals—that's right—a whole lot of JUNK!"

But SpongeBob paid no attention to Squidward. He was too busy making plans for his junk.

On Saturday, SpongeBob decided to take a break from organizing his junk collection to go jellyfishing with Patrick.

"I got one, Patrick!" shouted SpongeBob as he dropped his net on the creature.

"Uh, SpongeBob, I don't think that's a jellyfish," said Patrick. "It looks like a plastic bag."

"It *is* a plastic bag, Patrick!" SpongeBob said, almost as excited as if he'd caught an actual jellyfish. "This will be great for my collection! I can't believe I used to catch plastic bags and just throw them back. I can use this on my next shopping trip!"

"Wow," said Patrick. "I hope I catch a plastic bag. Sounds handy."

When SpongeBob got home from jellyfishing, he found his collection bins overflowing. Friends and neighbors had dropped off old hubcaps, flip-flops, toaster ovens, television sets, baby strollers, and some broken toys.

"These bins sure are a great idea, SpongeBob!" said a passerby as he tossed in an old vacuum cleaner.

SpongeBob was overwhelmed. It would take him a whole week to organize all of that new junk!

A few days later Mr. Krabs stopped by—but not to drop off junk.

"Lad, where ya been?" Mr. Krabs was panicked. "It's been days since you fried up a Krabby Patty! This junk collection is a great hobby, but you've got a heap o' hungry customers to feed, and I've got a pile o' money to start collectin'!"

"Don't worry, Mr. Krabs!" said SpongeBob. "I'm almost done organizing the new additions. I promise I'll report for duty right after I finish."

"I'll be expecting you," said Mr. Krabs. "On the double!"

But SpongeBob couldn't report to the Krusty Krab. His junk pile kept growing bigger and bigger until it was too big for his bins. He asked Sandy to help him replace them with supersize Dumpsters.

"Way to go, SpongeBob!" said Sandy. "This here recycling center is exactly what Bikini Bottom has always needed."

"What do you mean?" SpongeBob asked, confused. "*This* is a junk collection. What's recycling?"

"Recycling means separating leftover junk into bins—just like *you* did—and taking it to special processing centers where it can be made into something new! Recycling makes your surroundings look nice. It also saves sea critters from getting tangled in trash—or worse—mistaking trash for food, which can kill them."

SpongeBob's eyes grew big with horror. "You mean those sea creatures who shared their trash with me weren't playing with it?"

"I doubt it," said Sandy. "They were probably trying to get free."

Then a great light shined on SpongeBob.

"I *must* save Bikini Bottom from the perils of trash!" he declared.

So SpongeBob worked even harder. He collected more junk and trash, and sorted it day and night. By this point everyone in Bikini Bottom had heard about SpongeBob's recycling center. When the Dumpsters filled up, Sandy helped take them to the processing centers and then helped bring in new ones.

The harder SpongeBob worked, the more the trash piled up.

"You've got to slow down, little buddy," said Sandy. "This is too much work for one little guy."

"But, Sandy, I'm doing this for Bikini Bottom!" replied SpongeBob, frazzled.

Sandy started to worry. The next day she stopped into the Krusty Krab to see SpongeBob only to find out that he still hadn't come back to work. It had been two weeks! Finally she decided it was time to pay a visit to her friends at city hall and see if they could help.

SpongeBob continued to sort junk, but the junk was winning. Soon he found himself on top of a mountain of trash. He panted and sputtered. His eyelids and body drooped—even Squidward was worried.

"Look, SpongeBob," called Squidward from below. "Recycling is a good cause, but, uh, Mr. Krabs needs you, and I'm tired of doing all the work!"

SpongeBob just lay there with his eyes closed.

"SpongeBob?" called Squidward. "SpongeBob, quit joking around!"

But SpongeBob wasn't joking around. He was exhausted!

When he stirred, SpongeBob heard the roar of a crowd. He pinched himself.
"What's going on?" SpongeBob asked in a daze. "Am I a rock star?"
Sandy slapped SpongeBob on the back.
"No, little guy," said Sandy, laughing.
"Oh," said SpongeBob. "Then why is everyone in Bikini Bottom staring at us?"
"Turn around, SpongeBob," said Sandy. "You'll see!"

SpongeBob turned around and saw a building with his name on it. Inside there were three enormous Dumpsters, each with a different label: GLASS AND PLASTIC, ALUMINUM, and PAPER AND CARDBOARD. There was also a place to drop and swap junk that could be reused by someone else.

"Welcome to the grand opening of the SpongeBob SquarePants Recycling Center!" said Sandy.

The crowd cheered and applauded.

"But, Sandy," said SpongeBob. "I already *have* a recycling center."

"I know," said Sandy. "But this one will be run by the city of Bikini Bottom. I told the folks at city hall about your recycling project and they loved it. Now you only have to recycle your own stuff—and you can go back to your job at the Krusty Krab!"

SpongeBob thought for a moment.

"No more endless days of sorting junk in the blazing hot sun?" asked SpongeBob.

"That's right!" said Sandy. "And if everyone recycles, all those innocent sea critters will be safer *and* Bikini Bottom will look more beautiful than ever!"

"That's great!" SpongeBob cheered. "See, Squidward? I told you my junk would be worth something someday!"

THE SPONGEBOB SQUAREPANTS RECYCLING CENTER

PAPER

PLASTIC

"The city would also like to present you with this Green Medal of Honor," Sandy said, putting the medal around SpongeBob's neck.

"Wow," said SpongeBob. "Hey, Sandy, what does 'green' mean?"

"Green means you do your part to keep the world beautiful and healthy," said Sandy.

"Then you can call me Mister GreenPants!" cried SpongeBob.

Then SpongeBob thought for a moment. "Sandy, I wish everyone were green," he added

"You said it, little buddy," said Sandy. "I sure wish that too."

adapted by Erica David
based on the screenplay by Casey Alexander, Zeus Cervas,
Steven Banks, and Dani Michaeli
illustrated by Stephen Reed

It was a very special day for Mr. Krabs. "SpongeBob, me boy, I have something important to tell you," he said.

"What is it, Mr. Krabs?" SpongeBob asked.

"I've finally found a way to keep Plankton from stealing me secret Krabby Patty formula," Mr. Krabs replied. "I've sent it far, far away where he'll never be able to find it!"

"That's great, Mr. Krabs!" SpongeBob said. Then he frowned. "But we just ran out of Krabby Patties and we need the formula to make more!"

"Ah, tartar sauce!" Mr. Krabs grumbled. "The formula's all the way on the opposite side of the ocean!"

"I'll get it, Mr. Krabs," SpongeBob said. "Send me! I won't let you down."

"This is a very important mission, boy. The formula is in a safe-deposit box in the ocean's largest and safest bank, in Way Far-Out Townville," Mr. Krabs explained. He pulled out a key from his pocket. "This is the key to the box. Guard it with your life, SpongeBob."

"Aye, aye, sir!" SpongeBob said, determined to do his best.

Later that day, SpongeBob and Patrick boarded the Oceanic Express to go to Way Far-Out Townville. Little did they know that Plankton was following them.

"Remember, Patrick," SpongeBob said. "This is an important mission. Keep your eyes open for any suspicious characters."

SpongeBob and Patrick walked through the train to the dining car.

"Hey, SpongeBob, does that guy look suspicious to you?" Patrick whispered. "I think he might be spying on us!"

SpongeBob chuckled. Patrick was staring at his own reflection!

"Relax, Pat. I don't think *he* will give us any trouble," SpongeBob replied.

A man walked up to them. "I'm sorry, but the dining car is closed," he said in a snooty way.

"But we haven't even heard the specials yet!" SpongeBob said.

"No! The dining car is over for *you*. You must leave now!" the man snapped.

He grabbed SpongeBob and Patrick and tossed them out of the dining car.

"Well, that was certainly suspicious!" SpongeBob exclaimed. "Patrick, we'll have to find a safe place to store this for the night."

He reached into his pocket for the key, but couldn't find it! "The key! It's gone!" he yelled.

Just then, SpongeBob spotted Plankton. "Plankton, *you* stole the key!" he said.
"I just got here! I couldn't have stolen it . . . yet," Plankton said with an evil grin.
"I don't believe you. Search him, Patrick," SpongeBob ordered.
Patrick lifted Plankton up and shook him upside down. "He's clean," Patrick said.
"Then someone *else* on this train must have stolen the key!" SpongeBob said.

SpongeBob and Patrick called the police and rounded up the suspects.

"I think I know who did it," SpongeBob said. "Mr. Police Chief, I submit to you the nanny! Search this baby's diaper and you'll find the key."

The police chief searched—and found a stolen diamond in the baby's diaper!

"Great job, Mr. SquarePants! You nabbed the infamous Jewel Triplets Gang!" the inspector said.

"Hmm, if they didn't do it, then it has to be the butler," said SpongeBob. "The butler always commits the crime! Shake him down!"

When the police chief revealed that the "butler" had been wearing a mask, the cop exclaimed, "It's Oren J. Roughy! He's an international fugitive wanted for stealing more than seventy-five thousand dollars worth of ham sandwiches! Thank you, Mr. SquarePants!"

"You're welcome, but what about the key? I've failed Mr. Krabs!" SpongeBob wailed.

"Don't worry, it'll turn up," Patrick replied as he pulled something out of his pocket and began to pick his teeth with it.

"Patrick, that's the key! Where did you find it?" SpongeBob asked.

"I found it when I was cleaning your shorts earlier," Patrick answered.

"Oh," SpongeBob said sheepishly.

With the key found, SpongeBob and Patrick settled down for a nap. "Would you mind scooching over, SpongeBob?" Patrick asked. "I can't even move my eyebrows."

"I'm trying, Patrick, but it's really cramped. This isn't exactly Bikini Bottom!" SpongeBob said.

Suddenly Plankton popped up from under the covers. "Need more room?" he asked, opening the window. "Maybe I can help."

"What a cool view," Patrick said.

"Have a better look," said Plankton. Then he pushed SpongeBob and Patrick right out of the window. "So long. And thanks for the key!"

"What are we going to do, SpongeBob?" Patrick asked.
"Follow that train!" SpongeBob said.

They ran after the train until they came to the edge of a cliff. The train pulled away from them and followed the tracks into a canyon below.

"Uh-oh. Now what?" Patrick asked.

"Not to worry, Patrick. I have an idea," SpongeBob said. He grabbed Patrick and jumped off the side of the cliff.

"Ahhhhhhh!" Patrick screamed.

But SpongeBob just smiled as he flopped and flapped—and changed into the shape of a hang glider!

They soon landed safely on the roof of the train.

SpongeBob and Patrick climbed down into the train. They chased Plankton from one car to the next.

"You won't get away with this Plankton!" said SpongeBob.

Finally SpongeBob and Patrick chased Plankton all the way to the front of the train.

"All right, Plankton, end of the line!" SpongeBob cried.

"For you, maybe," Plankton replied as he quickly unhitched the engine from the passenger cars.

"Uh-oh, Patrick, we've got a big problem!" SpongeBob said. "We're on a runaway train!"

"Quick, look around. There has to be a way to stop this thing!" SpongeBob told Patrick.

Patrick stared at the control panel. He found a lever labeled BRAKE.

"Don't worry, SpongeBob, I'll save us!" he said. Patrick grabbed the lever and jerked it back and forth until it broke! He proudly showed SpongeBob the broken handle.

"Patrick, you broke the brake!" SpongeBob cried.

"It told me to," Patrick replied.

The train kept speeding down the tracks, and SpongeBob and Patrick were helpless to stop it! It burst through a train station and looped through the dreaded Twisted Trestles.

Meanwhile Plankton sneaked into the Way Far-Out Townville Bank. He used the key to open the safe-deposit box. "At last, my day of triumph has come!" he said.

As he picked up the Krabby Patty formula, a voice called out, "Just a minute, Plankton."

Mr. Krabs stepped out from the shadows. "Did you honestly think I wouldn't have planned for you?"

Plankton sighed as he handed over the formula. "Just keeping it warm for you, Krabs."

Suddenly they heard a rumbling sound. *Chugg-a, chugg-a, chugg-a, chugg-a!*

"What's that noise?" Mr. Krabs asked. When he turned to look, Plankton swiped the formula.

"Checkmate, Krabs! I win!" Plankton cried.

All of a sudden, a train smashed through the wall of the bank! SpongeBob and Patrick had arrived just in time. SpongeBob hopped down from the train and took the Krabby Patty formula from Plankton.

"Good job, boy!" Mr. Krabs said. "You saved the day!"

SpongeBob replied proudly, "I refused to fail, sir."

as told by anonymous sea-dwellers
book text based on the following screenplays: "Trenchbillies" and
"The Curse of the Hex" written by Aaron Springer & Richard Pursel;
"Welcome to the Bikini Bottom Triangle" written by Luke Brookshier, Nate Cash
& Dani Michaeli; "The Main Drain" written by Luke Brookshier,
Nate Cash & Doug Lawrence; "The Mountain Who Came to Bikini Bottom"
written by Aaron Springer & Dani Michaeli; and "Sponge-Cano" written by
Casey Alexander, Zeus Cervas & Derek Ivensen
illustrated by Dave Aikens

Far below the calm blue waters of the ocean lie many dark legends. The mere whisper of the word trenchbilly, a passing thought about the main drain, or the smallest suggestion of the Bikini Bottom Triangle would send chills down the spines of even the hardiest of sea creatures! No one dared to uncover these hidden mysteries. That is, until now . . . for none of those creatures could hold a candle to the bravest, yellowest sponge in the whole sea. And so SpongeBob SquarePants set off to uncover the six greatest legends of Bikini Bottom!

LEGEND #1: The Monster Who Came to Bikini Bottom

Patrick was playing in the ocean when he met a giant monster. Most people would have been terrified, but not Patrick! He and the monster became friends. They played with a snow globe and spent the afternoon laughing together.

Patrick brought the monster to meet SpongeBob. At first SpongeBob thought the monster was hurting Patrick.

This is even worse than yesterday when the ice machine broke at the Krusty Krab, thought SpongeBob. But then he realized that the monster was Patrick's new friend.

"And you are?" SpongeBob asked.

"Rarg!" the monster roared.

"Nice to meet you, Rarg!" SpongeBob replied.

But there was a small problem. Rarg didn't have anywhere to live in Bikini Bottom. Patrick offered him his rock, but Rarg was so big that Patrick's rock sat like a small hat on his giant head. The rock looked so funny on his head that SpongeBob and Patrick began to laugh and laugh. Suddenly Rarg picked the rock up and threw it as far as he could. Patrick's house was smashed into dozens of little pieces. Still SpongeBob, Patrick, and Rarg laughed even harder! It was so funny that Rarg began smashing more houses. He smashed SpongeBob's pineapple and Squidward's house, too!

Suddenly the police came to see what all the ruckus was about. When they saw Rarg, they built a fence around him to keep him in. But Rarg was too big for the fence. He just stepped right over it and started to run! The police chased him through the streets of Bikini Bottom, and just when they had him cornered, Patrick appeared.

"Wait just one minute!" Patrick cried. "He's my friend. Let me talk to him first."

Patrick and Rarg came up with a plan. Rarg now lives at the top of Bikini Bottom Alps and has a job. He supplies Bikini Bottom with all of their ice!

LEGEND #2: Welcome to the Bikini Bottom Triangle

Not too long ago strange things started happening in Bikini Bottom: SpongeBob's alarm clock went missing! So did Gary's shell, Squidward's clarinet, Patrick's cuff links—and even Mr. Krabs!

A sailor told them that legend says when an eerie fog rolls in, and the song of the mermaids is heard, things disappear into the Bikini Bottom Triangle—and they never come back! SpongeBob and Squidward searched high and low for Mr. Krabs when a fog rolled in, and mermaids began to sing. . . .

Suddenly Squidward and SpongeBob were sucked into a chute. They landed on a giant pile of discarded things—a gum-ball machine, a fridge, some tennis rackets, and even lawn mowers! A few moments later Patrick and Pearl came tumbling through the chute too.

Soon they found Mr. Krabs. He was having the time of his life. In fact he wanted to stay in the Bikini Bottom Triangle—until he thought that Plankton might be running the Krusty Krab!

SpongeBob and Patrick asked the singing mermaids for help.

"Look, we only know one thing. Nothing ever leaves the Bikini Bottom Triangle," they answered. "That's how we surround ourselves with cool new stuff. Anything beyond that is T.N.O.P.: totally not our problem."

They didn't care that SpongeBob and his friends were stuck.

But then Pearl told them that the mall had the best, coolest, most glitterishly fabulous new stuff. Now the mermaids wanted to go to the mall!

SpongeBob had an idea: If the mermaids sang their song backward, it might reverse the direction of the giant chute.

Instead of sucking things into the triangle, it would shoot everything inside back out.

It worked! Pearl and the mermaids immediately headed for the mall. And SpongeBob and Mr. Krabs discovered that the mysterious sailor had kept the Krusty Krab running the whole time they were gone!

"You've got a little vermin problem," said the sailor.

LEGEND 3: The Curse of the Hex

One dark and stormy night an old hagfish appeared at the Krusty Krab just as Squidward was locking up. She forced her way in, but Squidward refused to take her order. She just kept begging for a Krabby Patty, and Squidward and Mr. Krabs couldn't get her to leave. Then SpongeBob walked over to her and whispered something in her ear.

She finally agreed to leave but called out a warning.

"You haven't seen the last of me!" she yelled on her way out the door.

Later SpongeBob sneaked out of the Krusty Krab with two Krabby Patties for the hagfish. But as SpongeBob handed her the Patties, Mr. Krabs showed up and grabbed them first!

Angered, the hagfish shouted, "Eye of newt and frozen sharkskin slab, I hereby curse the Krusty Krab!" The next day no customers showed up at the Krusty Krab, and a mysterious fire burned some of Mr. Krabs' hard-earned cash! So he set off with SpongeBob to beg and plead with the hagfish to remove her awful curse!

The hagfish said she would lift the curse if they brought her the sacred gold doubloon from the throat of the giant golden eel. So SpongeBob led the way and retrieved the gold doubloon. The hagfish promptly used the coin for laundry.

"Finally!" she said.

Then they went to the Krusty Krab, and the hagfish pulled out a wooden CLOSED sign from in front of the restaurant. It wasn't a curse after all!

Relieved, Mr. Krabs and SpongeBob returned to work.

LEGEND 4: The Main Drain

Mr. Krabs once told SpongeBob and Patrick a scary story—the story of the main drain!

Mr. Krabs told them how two little boys many years ago stumbled upon a giant plug at the center of the ocean. They didn't know what it was, so they pulled on it. Suddenly everything was being sucked into the hole! Not only did the two kids go down the drain, but so did all of the houses and people of Bikini Bottom!

SpongeBob and Patrick decided to trek across the ocean to find the main drain to protect it. But when they got there, Patrick did not believe it was the real thing. They were about to pull the plug to make sure it was real when Mr. Krabs and Plankton showed up.

Mr. Krabs confessed that he and Plankton were the two kids in the story he told them, and he begged them not to pull the plug.

But Patrick accidentally pulled it and they were all sucked into the drain . . . along with all of Bikini Bottom!

Luckily, it was just a bedtime story!

LEGEND #5: Trenchbillies

One day SpongeBob and Patrick were chasing a jellyfish when they fell off a cliff down, down, down, until finally, they landed. *Hard.* Right on top of a trenchbilly! The trenchbilly dragged them to the leader, Ma Angler.

"As leader of this clan," she growled, "I must subject you to our clan initiation rites to see if you're worthy . . . of living!"

A trenchbilly walked up to them with his fiddle in hand, and he played a song. "SpongeBob, I think it's meant to be a musical challenge," Patrick whispered.

So SpongeBob grabbed a pair of suspenders and fastened them to his pants. Then Patrick picked up SpongeBob and began to strum on his suspenders like a guitar!

They passed the challenge—phew!

Next it was time for the hootin' and hollerin' contest. The trenchbillies' best singer, Betsy, yodeled the loudest, strongest yodel she could muster.

"What are we going to do?" SpongeBob asked.

"I don't know," Patrick answered. "But I sure am thirsty!"

Patrick opened a can of corn and began gulping. SpongeBob grabbed the can and gulped down the rest. Afterward they each let out the loudest, strongest burps ever!

The crowd went *wild!*

Next they were challenged to a wrestling match. But SpongeBob and Patrick showed everyone how to jellyfish instead. At first Ma Angler wasn't impressed, but then SpongeBob and Patrick jumped high into the air, collided, and collapsed on the ground. Ma Angler thought those were great wrestling moves, and she made them honorary trenchbillies!

She gave them each a set of trenchbilly teeth. A few moments later they learned that meant they'd have to stay there and take care of her forever! Hearing that, SpongeBob and Patrick ran as fast as they could back to Bikini Bottom where they belonged!

NOVELTY TEETH

LEGEND #6: Sponge-Cano

On a beautiful sunny day in Bikini Bottom, SpongeBob felt the urge to sing about all of the things he was grateful for. He was grateful for his house, his life in Bikini Bottom, and especially for his neighbor. Except his neighbor, Squidward, wasn't so grateful for all of that singing outside his window.

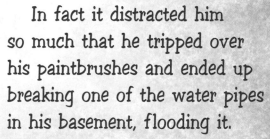

In fact it distracted him so much that he tripped over his paintbrushes and ended up breaking one of the water pipes in his basement, flooding it.

"I can give you a hand, neighbor!" SpongeBob said.

"No! You've done enough already!" yelled Squidward. "I don't want your help ever again!"

Realizing he was late for his job at the Krusty Krab, Squidward quickly fixed the water pipe and ran to work. But being at work didn't exactly change Squidward's attitude. He was grumpy and rude to the customers all day.

"This day couldn't get any worse," grumbled Squidward. "I'm the most miserable person in Bikini Bottom!"

Suddenly everyone heard a loud rumbling and could see fire raining down everywhere in Bikini Bottom. Mount Bikini Bottom had just erupted!

The town was in a panic! The raining lava was burning holes in everything—even through the roof of the Krusty Krab! It looked like Bikini Bottom was doomed!

That was until an ancient warrior, who had ruled over the ocean before the dawn of time, came to tell them how to stop it.

"To stop the volcano you must sacrifice the most miserable person . . . ," said the warrior.

Before he could finish speaking, the crowd began chanting, "Squidward! Squidward!" They tied him to a stake and carried him to the volcano. They were about to throw him in when . . .

"I am grateful for the life I have! Please help me, SpongeBob!" pleaded Squidward.

"You told me not to help you ever again," said SpongeBob.

Just then they heard another loud rumbling throughout Bikini Bottom—could it be another volcano? No, it was the pipe in Squidward's house exploding from the water pressure. The water blew the house into the air, and it landed right on the volcano. Bikini Bottom was saved!

"But you said the sacrifice had to be the most miserable person!" Squidward cried.

"No one let me finish," the warrior said. "I was going to say you must sacrifice the most miserable person's house to the volcano. No one ever listens to me!"

And so our brave SpongeBob survived and lived to tell about the legends of the deep . . . but not everyone is so lucky. Some never got out of the Bikini Bottom Triangle or even became trenchbillies. But now you know and can go out to uncover more hidden mysteries. What spine-chilling creatures will you discover?